Let's Motivate Ourselves

Flairs and Glairs

Publication House

Disclaimer

This is a work of fiction and solely represent the thoughts of the corresponding authors of the articles. Our editors have tried their best to edit the content of all the authors and check the plagiarism.

All the write-ups in this book are unique and are only published in this book.

In case any plagiarism or error is found, only the author is responsible alone, and not the publisher or the Compilers.

Cover Designing and Book Formatting
Shubham Shah and Ishani Agarwal

Acknowledgement

Firstly, I would like to thank my mom and dad for everything. Because I don't think without their constant support anything would be possible. Thank You So Much for believing in me. I will

try my level best to make you feel proud.

And yes, I especially thank all the well-wishers and my friends who were there for me in tough situations.

Thank You Very Much, Grishma Ninave Di for your constant support in every situation.

I am heartily grateful to our publishing team "Flairs and Glairs" for their understanding support in publishing this anthology.

Thank You So Much to Ishani Agrawal Di and Shubham Shah Bhaiya for giving me a chance to compile My Dream Anthology "Let's Motivate Ourselves".

And for always standing behind me like a pillar. Thanks a lot for your

love and support towards me.

And yes, how can I forget our talented co-authors.

The whole and soul of this anthology.

Thank you so much guys without you people nothing was possible.

Thank You who all believed in me............

Co Author

Shubham Shah (Founder Flairs and Glairs)
Ishani Agarwal (Co- Founder, Flairs and Glairs)
Manisha Sharma (Compiler)

1. Mohanapriya.K
2. Sahina Ghugha
3. Nivetha R C
4. Keerthana Suriya
5. Shubh Sayings
6. Krishna Motwani
7. Gaurav Sharma
8. Jayashree Sahoo
9. Devyani Neral
10. Diksha Motwani
11. Grishma Ninave
12. Sameer Bhatia
13. Mitali Bonde
14. Astha Priya
15. Alka Markand Mendhe
16. Harpreet Kaur
17. Shreya Pokhriyal
18. Reena Sharma
19. Agam Sachdeva
20. Archishman Satpathy
21. पलक जैन
22. Shivam Rai
23. Alisha Khan
24. Kirtika Bhatt
25. Supriya Mukherjee
26. Sneha Sathyanathan

27. Akash Chaurasiya
28. Anshika Dutt
29. Rabadiya Gopi D.
30. Sneha B. Mankar
31. J Vetri Michael Raj
32. Shaheen Ansari
33. Priyanka Varma
34. Rashmi Sri
35. Sakshi Jain
36. Ankitha P Menon
37. Ankita Dey
38. Sharmistha Kar
39. Ranu Manjhi 'Sanskriti'
40. Keerthana
41. Payal Kamdi
42. Harshita Verma
43. Ankita Nahar
44. Rahul Singh
45. Abhinav Sharma
46. Abhay Sinha
47. Somesh Kumar Jha
48. Khushi Patil
49. Ami Patel
50. Bhavika Dhiraj Sindhi

Shubham Shah

(Founder- Flairs and Glairs)

Shubham Shah, an entrepreneur at "Flairs & Glairs" a brand with dynamics in events organizing and cultural educational pan INDIA, is a 26yrs old guy who recently has entered the digital platform of imprinting emotions. He has initiated with his own open mic platform to help budding poets and aspiring writers under his brand named as "Teekhe Zasbaaat"

He is a commerce graduate from the Bhagalpur City of Bihar. He states Writing has impersonated him since childhood and he has now been writing for over a decade!

Cooking, on the other hand, is his passion! He also mentions, trying out new things just tickles him!

When asked sir, Why SPICY EMOTIONS?

He smiled and added, "agar jasbaat teekhe na ho toh wo jasbaat kahan" Spices are all that blends! So do his words!

As a chef, he presents to you his dish! Hot and freshly served! Taste it! Feel it! Enjoy it! You can also find his writing in the Book "Teekhe Zasbaaat" and 50+ Co-authored anthologies. With his passion to explore opportunities across Platforms, he is working with keen devotion and We wish him all the very best for his future ventures.

He is Featured in the International Magazine DeMode for his upcoming solo novel.

He is Approved by Ne8x for its Lit Fest, and is a Golden Star Awards 2020 Winner.

He is a India Book of Records Holder for his Anthology Satrang, and has the Grandmaster title by Asia Book of Records, for the same.

He has also been featured in Prabhat Khabar, Dainik Jagran, and a lot of other Newspapers in Bihar for his achievements.

He has been a proud co-author to

India Book Of Records (Title- Black)

World Book Of Records (Title -15 Wonders of Poetries)

India Book Of Records (Title - Aaina)

Vajra World Records Holder (Title - Gustakhi Maaf Hai)

High Range of Records Holder (Title - Gustakhi Maaf Hai)

Indian Book of Records

(Title - Road from Worst to Best)

Share your reviews on his

INSTAGRAM
@spicy_emotions
@shubham4shah
Or via email on
shubham2shah@gmail.com

To stay tuned to his work and opportunities follow his business Handles

INSTAGRAM   FACEBOOK   YOUTUBE

@flairsandglairs
@teekhezasbaaat

WEBSITE:
https://flairsandglairs.in/
https://flairsandglairs.com/

Ishani Agarwal

(Co-Founder- Flairs and Glairs)

Ishani Agarwal hails from the City of Joy, Kolkata.

She is the co-founder of her Community "Teekhe Zasbaaat" and Flairs and Glairs Publication.

Been a Compiler for 45+ Anthologies, she is in the process for more. Co-authored in 150+ Anthologies. She is a India Book of Records Holder, a Vajra World Records Holder, a High Range of Records Holder, an OMG Book of Records Holder, a Bravo Record holder, a Forever Star Book of World Records and an Indian Book of Records Holder.

Approved by Ne8x for its Lit Fest 2020, and Literary Icon 2020. Also a Golden Star Awards Winner 2020.

She has also been awarded with India Star Republic Award 2021, a part of She Awards by Awards Arc and Winner of Nari Samman 2021 by Literoma.

She is also selected as Best Achiever of the Year by AwardsArc and Most Challenging Compiler Award by Spectrum Awards.

She got her first solo Published,a solo Compilation consisting of first 750 contents of hers, titled "Hand That Burnt While Healing".

She has been featured by the National Magazine "Taree Zameen Par" with the title 'unstoppable'.

Also featured in the International Magazine DeMode for her upcoming solo novel, she is proud to write on social issues, and is happy with the love she is receiving.

Connect with her on Instagram: @Ishani_agarwal_quotes / @compilations_so_far

Manisha Sharma
(Compiler)

Here's

Manisha Vishnu Sharma. SHE AWARDEE 2021.

She is a poet and a writer from Nagpur, Maharashtra. Currently, she is pursuing B.Sc from Shivaji Science College, Nagpur.

She loves to write and perform her poetry's in Open Mic Events too. She has a fond of arts and craft's works. Currently, working as a Project Head At The Opus Coliseum.

She has worked as a co-author in 13+ anthologies. Her First Debut Book was "Whimsical Motions". Also, She is compiler of 3 anthologies and more are in progress.

Connect with her on Instagram: - @damaged.pen
Email ID: - manishasharmangp@gmail.com

आखिर क्यूँ?

किसी के नाखुश करने से,
तुझे क्यूँ फरक पड़ रहा है!
खुद को खुश करने की उम्मिद, तू खुद से लगा...
तू दूसरों से उम्मिद क्यू रख रहा है?

तू तो अकेला आया था ना,
अकेला भी जी सकता हैं!
फिर क्यू दिखावे वाले प्यार के लिए...
तू दर दर भटक रहा है?

जो तेरा हैं, वो तेरा होगा।
अगर वो चला गया, तो तेरा कैसे?
और जब वो तेरा है ही नही, तो फिर तू क्यू...
किसी और की अमानत के लिए यूँ तड़प रहा है?

तू इंसान है, माना मैने!
पर फिर तू क्यू!
सब प्राणियों से ज्यादा दिमाग होने पर भी,
तू अंधेरे मे रहना पसंद कर रहा है?

Don't Wait For Anyone; Be There For Yourself.

If you need someone, be there for yourself. If you want something, be able to get that thing by yourself for yourself. If you want anyone to decide for you, be wise enough to take decisions for yourself. If you want to go somewhere, be strong enough to go alone by yourself.

In the whole universe, we all are the luckiest creatures that we have got a beautiful life to live. Don't waste it on things which are worthless. Stop wasting time and take stand for yourself when needed. Stop wasting energy and invest it in something useful and worthful for yourself.

Dream big as well as small, no matter what.
Keep working to make your dreams true and to make yourself better, more worthy, more beautiful.

And when you will create the life you want. That is where, you will find real happiness.

Mohanapriya. K

Co-author Mohanapriya.K is a good writer from Tamilnadu, India. She has completed her Bachelor's degree in Engineering stream. She has been a writer for one year as her passion. She wants to be a best compiler in future. She is very happy to undertake such noble art. Yet she sincerely hope that this writing journey of her will continue as sweetly as it is now and will bring her many successes.

I.G : @colours_honey_official

E-mail : doraa.kutty@gmail.com

Don't Forget To Motivate Yourself

We do not know when or what will happen in our life. The next minute is a life of uncertainty. So learn to live the life you live in peace and happiness. You are the top most priority for you. Don't lose yourself for anyone. Anyone can change anyway but the relationship between you and you will never change. We need some people to encourage and support us everywhere and in every situation. But more important than that is the support we give ourselves. You have to motivate yourself more than others do. Motivate others! Motivate Yourself! No matter what happens to us. We must not lose our self-confidence and courage. Whatever the situation, just shine like a pearl. Just live who you are. Let your poetry rain down and your thoughts and thoughts overflow and flow like a waterfall. Your self-confidence and inner trust on you give you wings.

Trust Yourself In All The Situations

For that, do not finish the process halfway. Yes, a good start is a good end - they say. But everything that happens in this world depends on our hard work and effort. So the beginning can be anyway, but we hope its end will be a good one. Because that decision depends on the time too. Love, caring, Warmth, affection get used to living with these love to love avoid being hatred. Never be afraid of retribution, sarcasm etc. Do not be afraid to stop your trips to victory. Because you know they are not true. If so why should you fear for them or why should you regret thinking about it. Speakers are a thousand, why? Lakhs, even crores will speak reproach about you. Those who slander you today will praise you with the same mouth when you see many of you praising her verbally when you are in a better position tomorrow. Because they only know how to speak.

Sahina Ghugha

Sahina Ghugha, 20-year-old B.Com student at Saurashtra university Rajkot. She is from Jamnagar city of Gujarat. She is state level winner in poetry competition 2017. She is Co-author of 10+ anthologies. She is an amazing writer and poet and she wants do something for society through her pen. Insta ID:- Itz_Sahina_write

तू आग है कड़कती ठंडी की,
तू ठंडक तपती गर्मी की
मिट्टी है तू उस बारिश की
जो फैलती खुशबू चारो ओर है

तू ख़ाक है जो कहलाती भभूत
तू राख है जो बहेती पवित्र
तु राग है उस रागिनी का
सुनाई देता जो हर हर दौर है

तू खून है अपने शूरवीर पूर्वजों का
मिट्टी तुझ में बसी मातृभूमि की
कर दिखला तू आज कुछ ऐसा
उग निकला हो जैसे नया भोर है

Nivetha R C

Nivetha R C, a young poetess from Coimbatore, Tamil Nadu. She graduated BA English Literature from PSGR Krishnammal College for Women. Currently, she is pursuing MA English in KSG College of Arts and Science, Coimbatore. She started writing poems from the age of 13. She used to write in Tamil and English. Nivetha likes to personify the things around her and tries to reveal its emotions through her words. She is interested to deliver the unheard conversations between two non-living things.

My Mirror To Me

Dear Girl,
I don't want anyone to
depend on you.
Neither I want you to depend on others...
If you want to love come to me
Talk with me
My love for you
is real and hurt less.
No matter what,
Remember to smile always.
Love yourself,
because it will be with you forever.
Not many, maybe not even a single one will believe in you.
But it doesn't matter.
Always remember to
keep 'You' as your first priority
Follow your passion.
It doesn't matter who leaves your life.
What does matter is you don't leave your passion.
No matter whether you cried,
failed, broken or alone.
What does matter is your attempt.
Attempting itself is greater than break down.

Me And My Wall

Sometimes
I wondered where is a door in the wall
to enter the world that I longed for.
You arrested me.
You showed the obstacles in front of me.
Which is in the form of restricted society.
Every single brick in you
revealed my fears and weakness.
That is working against my desires.
I watched you again.
And I realized who you are.
Yes, you are a mirror of my inner self.
And then I went a few steps forward as a new person with confidence.
That moment you were broken into pieces and I entered my world.
Yes, you are not a wall
You are a mirror to my inner self.

Keerthana Suriya

She is Ms.KEERTHANA SURIYA a highly aspired, dynamic medical student, social-worker, a passionate writer and classical dancer who is engaging in self and social development, building relationships and exhibiting integrity. She is Co-Author of various other anthologies. She is Founder of WACHC Foundation – Women And Children Health Care and also holding the position of Women's Health Empowerment Project Head in the trust Women's Renaissance Centre. She strongly believes that

Don't Walk Away From Negative People

Self-motivation is not that easy
But it is essential for success
Be positive towards yourself,
and interact in positive ways
with those around you.
It is not realistic to feel energized 24/7
Sometimes you need to unplug
yourself from work to
charge yourself with motivation
Pause for few minutes
and dream about success.
If you dream it you can do it
Most importantly to stay motivated,
don't walk away from negative people
I repeat!
Don't walk away from negative people
RUN RUN RUN

Shubh Sayings

SHUBHSAYINGS Is into writing, he writes by heart and expresses it in his words. He likes writing short quotes about his view LIFE by his own experiences.

The Point Here Is Perfectly Connected To Your "Inner Peace"

Life is too short to hold something up for someone but at the same time life is too short to just sit and wait for opportunities, you need to let go of things or people in your life if you feel they are not allowing you to let yourself free. Point here is to " improve , improve together & grow , grow together."

Don't let anyone cage you and be a barrier between you & your dreams. Just let go of something or someone who doesn't want you grow. At the end of the day when you achieve your dreams , you will be left with few people but they will be the only real people in your life. So definitely celebrate your dreams but more than that celebrate the real people you earned journey .

In this amazing journey.

Self-Motivation

Jab sahi hoga tu,
Galat tab samja jaega
Shaurat se bahut badega tu,
Lekin khudh ko akela paaega
Yahi to zindegi hai mere yaar
Kabhi taarefe paaega,
Toh kabhi badnaam hojaega
Bahut mehnat lagti hai kuch hasil karne
Me isley dikhane se katrata nahi ..
Bahut dua lagti hai kaabil banne me,
Isley un farishto ka naam lena bhulta nahi.
Kaafi logo ne madat nahi ki,
Lekin mai madat karne se peeche hatuga nahi
Bahut aage jauga ek din,
Lekin haarne se daruga nahi
Sunhare aksharo me naam likha jaega mera ek din,
 lekin zamin par pair rakhna bhuluga nahi.
Kitni bhi mushkil aaye toh kya baat hai kehna
Kitni bhi mushkil aaye toh kya baat hai kehna

"ZINDEGI BAHUT KHOOBSURAT HAI MERE YAAR
YU HI HASTE REHNA"

Krishna Motwani

Krishna Motwani is a Student currently. She use to pen down her feelings. She is a moody girl. She started writing in the month of june,2020. She writes in her free time. She writes some motivational quotes or poetries too and practices artworks also. She lives her life like a bird As bird flies freely and enjoys life like that she also lives her life freely and enjoy fullest. For motivating and inspiring poems and quotes.

You can check her on instagram : @ unique__blog_

You Can Do It!

Like a moon, use to glow always,
A new chance will come to find your best ways.
Let's have a new hope again,
Let's forget that past's pain.
Let's start a new journey! Right!
Let's hug our life tight!
We are getting chance to do something new again,
Let us forget dark phases and start again!
Let's have more love with nature,
Let's make our heart pure.
Remove all of the stress and start,
Let's do it! Your strength is with you in your heart!

Gaurav Sharma

Co-author Gaurav Sharma is a good writer from Kaman Bharatpur. He has completed his 12th std in science stream. He has been writing poetry for 7 year .years as his passion. He wants to be a lawyer in future.

सकारात्मक सोच रखोगे तो सब काम आसान जाएंगे
सकारात्मक रही सोच तो आप महान हो जाएंगे
सकारात्मक सोच रखो तो मंज़िल भी मिल ही जाती है
ओर कोशिश की जाए तो दीवार भी हिल ही जाती है वैज्ञानिकों ने
तूफान को नापने का उपकरण बनाया है
यह सकारात्मक सोच ही तो है जिसने ये कर दिखाया है
सकारात्मक सोच से तो दुनिया भी बदली जा सकती है
ओर 60 % वाले कि भी अच्छी रैंक आ सकती है
सकारात्मक सोच से मिल जाते है समस्या के सब हल
फिर हमेसा करोगे आज कभी ना कहोगे ये करूँगा कल
परीक्षा खराब जाए तो कोई भी निराशा ना हो
अगला अच्छा हो बस यही आशा होनी चाइये
देखो प्रयास हर बार करूँगा
पिछली गलतियों मैं सुधार करूँगा

Jayashree Sahoo

Jayashree Sahoo is habitant of ODISHA. Her writings started on yourquote, notojo and mirakee like writing platforms. You can search her on yourquote by name of Jaya Jayashree . Nowadays She is member of many writing communities and earned a alots of certificates through her writings . She is Co-author of 160+ anthologies .Also She is Compiler of many anthologies in Hindi ,English and Odia languages . Currently She is working as project head and board member of a reputed publication.

Learning from life,
Let life make me sad
I wish everyone well
I will be happy with the love of others
I will love more than I need to

That I can do something for the country
I asked for life permission
Winning everyone's trust in life
I can fight with the world

I will fight the battle of life
There will be victory in the world struggle
I will endure all the hardships of life
I will give a new look to the world

Crossing the Ankabanka road of life
I'll start fixing the world
I will make the relationship a life of freedom
Forgetting the world in fear of death

A life full of darkness
Pride without others
Happy with everyone
By eliminating the scattering of the mind

Concerned neo-hippies and their global warming, i'll tell ya
Stay away from all greed and don't worry
Where the journey of life begins
It's all about moving forward without backtracking
The subtle subtleties give Sudhir life
I will not call on God without despair
The subtle soul of the happy world
Man has his own soul

Devyani Neral

She is a co-author of 50 anthologies and a published poet .24 years of her age has given her innumerable thoughts to write. She is an engineer by profession and a writer by passion. Reading thrills her and feels her with joy and so does writing. She is currently writing her first book which will be of self-help genre. Motivational writings are her cup of tea. She strongly believes that we are here to write our own story and create our own path.

Lost But Found

I am lost in a crowd,
where no one recognises me.
Seems that sun will debar me from its sunshine.

But why do you want to be found?
Why do you want someone else's recognition?
Why can't you find yourself within you?

It's up to you to grab that sunshine.
It's up to you to recognise yourself.
It's up to you to bloom in that crowd.
And finally, it's up to you to shine in the sunshine.

Edge Of Blade

Poem Of A Pencil With Sharpener.

I can write billions of words.
But who will write about me?

Who says, pain will lower you?
Ask me the secret of my edge.

Fallen particles will narrate my story.
Scrap will depict my life.

On the edge of blade, I sharpen myself.
Glance at me. You will see my sharpness.

No matter how much hardships you face, you will rise
and will write a new story again.

Should I blame the blade for the pain ?
Or should I praise the blade for the edge?
Choice is yours.!!

Diksha Motwani

Diksha Motwani is a passionate girl from Mumbai, Maharashtra. She loves to pen her feelings. She is introvert but her pen makes her extrovert. She is a writer, singer, artist and a poet!

<u>मत हार तू।</u>

ए मेरे टूटे हुए दिल,
क्या मिला तुझे प्यार करके?
क्या मिला प्यार का इज़हार करके?
क्यों अब रो रहा?
क्यों अब तक इंतजार कर रहा?
क्यों आज भी उस ही को चाह रहा?
क्यों अपनी रातों की नींद उड़ा रहा?
क्यों उसको पाने के लिए खुद को खो रहा?
बस अब चुप होजा,
थोड़ी देर ठहर जा,
तुझे उसको भुलाना होगा,
तुझे खुदको ताकतवर बनाना होगा,
तुझे वह शायद भूल चुका,
वह शायद किसी और का हो चुका,
हस्ले अब तो,
जीले ज़िन्दगी अब तो
 काश वह समझ पाता,
काश मैं उसको बता पाता,
ए दिल, कुछ सोच अपने बारे में,
भूल जा उसे,
क्यों अपनी रातों की नींद उड़ा रहा
उसके लिए जिसे शायद ही तेरी परवाह है,
जिसे पता ही नहीं की तू उसे कितना चाहता है।
चल अब सोजा,
अपने सपनों में खोजा,
नींद तेरी आती ही होगी,
बंद कर आंखें,
सोजा आराम से।

Grishma Ninave

Grishma Ninave was born and brought up in the Orange City, Nagpur. She is a Science graduate and an avid reader. Thriller is her favourite genre. Currently working as a Project Head at Flairs & Glairs Publication House. Published in the Editorial section of a national magazine as Aaj Ki Womaniyaa, in the first edition of 2021. A firm believer that happiness is not something that you find, it's something that you create. She loves travelling, blogging and listening to music.

Why?

You are the mother of your desire,
To them, within you, no one can abort.
Above every worldly pleasure lies what you aspire,
All you need is your own support.

Sow good and you attain good,
Is what Primary School had taught.
But why did you still withstood,
All the injustice that your enemies brought?

Watering weeds will never turn,
The into sweet fruiting plants.
Then why did you not spurn,
There negative enchants?

Lead Your Life The Way You Wish...

Why do you look around for validation,
When it is going to cause nothing but aberration.
Go ahead and grab your niche,
Lead your life the way you wish...

Crying for the promise that wasn't kept,
Why their flaws do you not accept.
Just make plans and work to accomplish,
Lead your life the way you wish...

Why do you get affected when they look at you pitiably,
One day you too shall be ignorant, probably.
My friend, do not embrace anguish,
Lead your life the way you wish.

It's their fault that they are so subhuman,
But do not cry went to you they abandon.
Negative thoughts from your mind you banish,
Lead your life the way you wish.

Sameer Bhatia

Born on February 27th 1965 in a musical family, Sameer is a composer musician and a music teacher by profession. Around 40 years of varied experience in music field, Sameer has an inclination towards writing songs and creating music. His tremendous experience ignited his passion towards writing poetry. His poetries (both in English and Hindi) are mainly being inspired by the spectrum of human emotions. As he says he is voice of a common man.

IG - sameerdilse_poetry ; Youtube - Sameerdilse

Yesterday when GOD appeared in my dreams
Everything was exactly the way that it seems

I asked Almighty to bless me with good fortune
He said blow your own trumpet to get the right tune

Oh God, I want to get success, so please let me know the
right address
God told me to climb the mountain hard work to reach the
destination success

Oh God I'm desperate to get the fortune my way
So please help me God, the time is running away

God said,
You're fully equipped Oh mankind
This is the way I have designed

Your fortune is in your own hands
Unfortunately, no one understands

You will reap whatever you have sown
You don't get fortune; you make our own

Change yourself and fortune will change
I know you might find it strange

I thought within my mind…

To reach the stars and moon
I have to blow the right tune
To see myself up there soon
I 've to make my own fortune

Mitali Bonde

Mitali Bonde lives in Nagpur and is still going through college. She enjoys reading very much as it is a way to lose oneself in someone else's mind! She believes that poems are a way for everyone to feel myriads of emotions!

All Will Be Fine!

You fall,
It's not bruises that hurts it's the heart,
But that someone was never there to pull you up from the
start,
It's not your fault you couldn't see the truth,
No matter what... No matter all alone you have your back.

A new beginning with tears,
Yes, they would come...but soon you would laugh with no
fear.
Spreading your wings, you would fly,
No matter what... No matter the memories,
You have all the time to make new ones,
To be what you couldn't be before,
To be truly happy for yourself to be as happy as u were
before!

Motivation

When hopes are high, it makes you sly.

The burden is so big, it takes a lot of energy to hold it.

The night darkens with every step that time you have to halt
and check.
You get support which you want,
But it's hard to move on in different font.

Time runs so fast, Leaving you downcast.

Will is there but not the determination,
It keeps you wanting and in tension.

Miracles happen everywhere, making you think Life is fair.
Sometimes problems seem so simple,
But it takes lots of determination to move on with a dimple.

Then it is frustration which you call,
And move on to bad things when you fall.
Life is not that simple as you say it is full of
unpredictable things at the bay.
Sometimes you go through darkest of times....
But just remember every morning there is sunlight.

Astha Priya

Astha Priya is a 21 years old girl with keen observation towards life and optimism. She is into literature very much. For more than 7 years, she has been writing in her own space. Few incidences and experiences led her to write.Then she decided to get a platform for writing and made her Instagram WRITE-UP page @scribbled_solace. She believes that the person who loves its own soul the most, can only radiate love to others too.

Make Yourself The Very First Priority

To all the people struggling with their identities and relationships, I want to tell them that choose your own self first because that's where the game changes. No matter what happened till date, no matter how many times you've been taken for granted, just start over again. Lock everything back there and move forward. Search for the life you've always wanted and make it possible. Love yourself the way you love others. Take a little break from things that are overwhelming, say NO to things that you don't want to do, cry your heart out over things that's troubling your sanity, because self-care is important. You need to give yourself time. It's okay to ask for a break, it's okay to get isolated for a while. Do whatever makes you happy. Stop trying to please others coz that's not gonna happen ever. Instead make yourself happy because when you're happy your soul is at peace and it'll radiate positive vibes and that'll eventually make everyone happy around you. So, don't forget to smile before distributing one.

Let Go Of People And Things That Are Beholding Your Growth

It happens with all of us once in a while, when someone treats us like we are one of many options. Don't let them make you feel demeaned, just walk out. Trust me you need to know your worth and what you have to offer to others. Never settle for anything less than you deserve and if you're not getting that you need to let go because it's definitely not worth it. People will call it your ego or pride but you need to remember it's not, it's your self-respect. It's your love and concern for your own individuality. It's okay to take care of yourself more than anything else coz we all lose ourselves in course of loving others and that's wrong. Coz at the end of the day you stand alone for yourself. And most importantly, let go of your past coz what's done is done. You still have a life to shape. I will finish my words with a micro poem of mine—

"AS HANDS OF CLOCK TICKED
I WISHED IT TO STOP
COZ I WANT AN ETERNITY WITH MYSELF"

Alka Markand Mendhe

She is Alka Markand Mendhe. A girl from Gondia district of Maharashtra. She is writer with soft heart who feels every little thing. She is emotional and sensitive which can be seen in her write-ups . She wants to publish her solo book one day . You can follow her on Instagram - @thepenstories 134 & YourQuote - alka134

जो मेहनत करते हैं,
वो कभी शिकायत नहीं करते
वो किस्मत पर नहीं,
ख़ुद पर यकीन करते हैं !

अपने मंज़िल को पाने का रास्ता
वो खुद बनाते हैं,
उम्मीद दूसरों से कम खुद से ज्यादा करते है
वो किस्मत पर नहीं ख़ुद पर यकीन करते हैं !

वक़्त कैसा भी वो सही वक़्त का इंतजार नहीं करते,
बिना मेहनत किए वो कभी हार नहीं मानते,
जो मेहनत करते है ,
वो किस्मत पर नहीं ख़ुद पर यकीन करते हैं !

उड़ते पंछी को आसमान के ओर जाते देखा
तो सोचा की आसमान कितना अच्छा हैं
फिर सोचा की कुछ देर बाद उसे भी तो वापस
जमीन पर ही आना है....
ऊंचाइयों को छूकर वो जमीन को कहा भूलता है
उडले चाहे जितना वो अपने घर जमीन पर ही लौट आता है,
ना घमंड है उसे ऊंचाइयों पर उड़ने
का ना अफ़सोस है उसे वापस अपने घर लौट आने का,
वो पंछी भी हमें कितना कुछ सीखा जाता है,
आसमान में जाकर भी वो अपने घर को कहा भूलता है ।

उडलो जितना उड़ाना है इसमें गलत कुछ नहीं
अपने सपनों को हकीकत के पंख दो खुद को
भी ऊचे आसमान में उड़ने का मौका दो...
बस ये याद रहे कि जितना भी ऊपर चले जाए
अपने पैरों को जमीन पर ही रहने दो...
जितना भी ऊपर चले जाओ
बस अपने घर जाने का रास्ता याद रखो...!

Harpreet Kaur

Harpreet Kaur; She is a poet and writer. She has done M.Sc.(Physics) from Punjabi University, Patiala, Punjab. She loves to write and explore her deep feelings through her poetry. She likes to play guitar and read books in her free time.

Connect with her on Instagram: - @preet__07

Quest

She is seeking path
She is looking around
But don't know it's within
Only her powers are bound

True Path

I follow the path told by people to see the sunshine...
But in the end i realized it is nowhere but is present in the
heart of mine...

Shreya Pokhriyal

Shreya Pokhriyal is a college student who lives in Dehradun and persuading her career as a writer is been 1 year. She loves exploring and learning new things. She is too small but started her career a way in 2019 by joining as a co-author in the book name 'Faded Memories'. It's her first anthology. She has been worked in 100+ anthologies. Her Instagram handle is @An_anomalous_poet. The anthologies I had worked on are as follows Petrichor, Amor Patriae, next level attitude, Valentine's week book, logbook of 2020 and many more.

Never Give Up

If you really own it...wanna live with it don't ever quit on that. It can be your career, your dreams, a person in your life...or anything you want to own, please don't quit.

And in my opinion, if you really own it no one can stop you to be with that, it's you only whose creating such damn reasons, always criticizing or to believe yourself to be in that situation…

If you quit on something you love, which basically shows that you are partially in love with that because love does not allow the inner self to leave something you love in the hardships…

Actually, love is not the part of yours, it's you only....

Many of us will say this thing is will be a bullshit but its truth.

Bright Future

Just because my heart is full,
There's always a room for more,
A bundle of new contingent.
Soon arriving at my door.
A little ball of small fire,
Which will never let me tired.
More than a ball of joy,
An active little girl who dreams,
But never screams.
Walking in her father's footsteps,
A simpatico for all tools,
And following her own rules.
Which makes her still away from all fools.
First made me know you,
For making a family of three or four.
Now I have everything I had desired,
Soon a bright future will come to me.

Reena Sharma

वह श्रीमती रीना शर्मा हैं वह दिल्ली में रहती हैं। वह एक गृहणी हैं उन्हें कविता, कहानियां और उद्धरण लिखना बहुत प्रिय लगता है। उन्होंने अभी कुछ ही समय से लिखना शुरू किया है इसी लॉकडाउन में। वह एक सकारात्मक विचारों वाली लेखिका हैं और वह अपनी लेखन प्रतिभा को सब तक पंहुचना चाहती हैं। वह एक प्रेरणा दायक लेखिका हैं।

तू कायर नहीं हैं

जो चाही है मंज़िल मैंने उस तक लड़ कर ही जाया जाएगा,
मुसीबत लाख़ आए पथ पर उन सबको मात दे जाएगा,
सफलता चाहते हो तो कोई बड़ा लक्ष्य तो चुनो,
सोच को बड़ा करो किसी बात से मत डरो,
लोग हंसेंगे तुम पर पर तुम ख़ामोश रहो,
जवाब उनको वक़्त देगा तुम अपना काम करो,
सफलता पाने निकले हो तुम तुम्हें ही जितना होगा,
आत्म विश्वास के साथ हिम्मत का ढोल पीटना होगा,
जल्दी सफलता पाने के चक्कर में मत करना कभी गलती,
देर से ही सफलता मिले तो सफलता भी होगी उतनी ही बड़ी,
हिम्मत कुछ करने से आएगी तू अपना मन तो बना,
बिना कुछ किए पत्ता भी नहीं हिलता बिना
कुछ किए सत्ता भी नहीं मिलती,
तू एक बार आसमां की और देख
और उड़ जा,
तू कायर नहीं है चल उठ और सबको बता।

बदलेगी ज़िन्दगी एक दिन
चल ज़िन्दगी एक नई शुरुआत करते हैं
तुझे और भी कुछ ख़ास करते हैं
आगे निकल गए सब हम पीछे रह गए,
ज़िंदगी की कश्ती में पतवार बह गए,
आते रहते हैं ज़िन्दगी में उतार चढ़ाव,
हर एक लम्हे का अलग आंनद लेते हैं,
होता अलग अलग हुनर सब में है,
उसे पहचानने की काबीलियत सब में नहीं,
रखो ख़ुद पर विश्वास करना है
कुछ ख़ास,
बनने अपने रास्ते ख़ुद हैं,
बढ़ाते रहना है अपने कदमों को,
ना रुकना है ना झुकना है,
बदलेगी ज़िन्दगी एक दिन जो तुमने सोचा है।

Agam Sachdeva

She is an extremely talented girl with a very beautiful mind. She writes so well at such a young age. Though, she is just 14 years old but still is adored by many people. She has been a part of many anthologies earlier and has made her parents proud. She is a beautiful creation of God.

Don't Quit

When things go wrong as they sometimes will,
When the road you are on, will seem like a hill.
When your savings are low and expenditure is high,
When you want to smile, but you have to sigh,
When the love is pressing you down a bit,
You may take rest, but don't you quit.

Nobody knows when failure turns into success,
And then you can okay and to all your things have access.
It may seem near to you when it is afar.
So, stick to tight when yoy on the hardest hit.
But make sure, you don't quit.

Make A Promise To Yourself

Promise yourself to be strong,
Promise yourself that nothing will disturb your peace of mind.
And you not just to other but to yourself will be kind.
Will not keep any fake smile on your face,
Otherwise, I will be the one who will trace.
Dear, I know we are on a life's race
But don't worry.
Promise yourself to take care of yourself
And no matter what, on your good doing appreciate and clap.
Be an optimist and create all your good doing list.
And instead of getting bored,
Enjoy the mist,
Promise yourself,
You will be your greatest motivation and world's one of the best creations.

Archishman Satpathy

Archishman Satpathy, often called the Enthusiast Writer is a young dynamic writer from Deogarh, Odisha. He is presently pursuing B.Tech from IIIT Bhubaneswar. He started writing Quotes and Short Poetries from a young age of 16 and had now made it as his passion. He has contributed as co-author in more than 180 anthologies. He is the author of the book "LAKEEREIN ZINDAGI KE".

Jewel In Us

Without specialities, we are not here
We all have something hidden jewel
The only need of the hour is to explore
Have we ever thumped our back in
and Said that I did my best or well done
Definitely not because of we are not sure
That even we have some capabilities
Penning this I am feeling shame on us
Just because we are so called humans
And still unable to use our conscience
We are well educated as called by some
We are even aware of the mishaps but
Still unable to think and research properly
To understand that even we can do
That ordinary fellows can never also
Even we have some thirsty potential
For which some successful people
Have sacrificed half of their lives also
Just the need is to believe in yourself
I started loving myself, upto you now

We Will Be The Great

Is the need for Success an addiction
Or it is a zeal of the self-depressed heart
Can you please recite the worm hole poem
Of your name included with link of great
As a divine flier you are sending the mails
To your inner self in much needed esteem
Have you ever stop behaving like machine
Just once you achieved and thought it luck
Never thought for luck, hard work even suck
Losing the patient can't you care the rest
And feel the much-needed sacrifice and pain
For a short-term pleasure and dude strange
Can't you make a life enjoyable levelled best
For any achievement so huge for thinking
Can't you stop dwelling the worst in rest
Can't you give up all those stopping you
From achieving that very bloody zeal
If not then stop thinking now and start moving
forward to the zion of hopes anyway
May be your will win or you will be the great

पलक जैन

इनका नाम पलक जैन है। ये आस्था शास्त्री के नाम से भी जानी जाती है। इनका जन्म 15 सितम्बर 2000 का है। ये अपनी पढाई जैन दर्शन और संस्कृत विषय से उदयपुर (राज.) से पूरी कर रही है। ये शाहगढ , सागर, (मप्र) की रहने वाली है। ये अपने गायन के क्षेत्र में प्रमुख गायिका है।। ये बच्चो मे उच्च संस्कारो को पिरोने का कार्य शिविर आयोजित करके बहुतायत करती है। ये वर्ष 2009 से लेखन का कार्य कर रही है। इनकी इक पुस्तक "काया का साया" कार्यरत है।

हताश न हो मुसाफिर,
तू खुद तेरे साथ है ।
अश्कों का दरिया तो हर किसी का गहरा है ,
बस तू यही आस-पास है।

आरोपों के लफ्ज
तुझे रोक नहीं सकते ।
इन खालिदों के नजरिए,
तुझे कचोट नहीं सकते ।

"दोस्त हो फाजिल
पर मुकर गया तेरा साथ ।
तू न समझ भीड़ में अकेला,
थाम ले बस खुद का हाथ ।

प्यार मोहब्बत दोस्ती यारी
या हो कोई रिश्तेदारी ।
ताकत लगा अब तेरी बारी,
सोच बस ये है दुनियादारी ।

हूँ बाकिफ तेरी मुस्कान से,
दर्द भरे अश्कों की परछाई है।
तो भी हँसती रह इन ओठों से,
 समझ ये तेरे गमों की रिहाई है।
शिद्दत से दे तू हर इम्तिहान ,
मेहनत की है.रंग तो लाएगी।
खाली हाथ नहीं जरा देख तेरा अंजाम,
खुशियाँ नहीं तो गम तो लाएगी।

शीशा

छलावा काने पर डाँट लगा दे,
तेरी नजरों से तुझे मिला के.
तेरे मुखौटा तुझे दिखा दे,
वह शीशा ही तो है।

अकेलेपन में साथ दिला दे.
गफलत से रूबरू हरादे
धोखे का अहसास करा दे
वह शीशा ही तो है

छिपा दरिया का वो मोती बता दे ,
मासूमियत से गुफ्तगू करा दे।
खुदको तेरा हमदर्द बना दे
वह शीशा ही तो है , तेरा प्रतिबिंब ही तो है ।

Shivam Rai

Shivam Rai is a College Student doing His Bachelors in Arts, Completed Higher education by stream science. Writing is Once his hobby at starting but it become his passion today. He loves to write poetries about many different kinds of topic. He is the admin of page Emotions_have_sound on Instagram and Facebook. He also have a Channel on YouTube named (Emotions Have Sound) where He Has putted some of His lovely and amazing write ups. So if you are a poetry lover must take a look of it.

लड़ना प्रारंभ कर

यदि शिखर कि उचाईयों पर चाहते हो खुदको,
तो ख्वाहिशें छोड़ कोशिशों का आरंभ करो
सोये ज़मीर को फिर जगा, लड़ना प्रारंभ करो।

आपसि रंजिशों में यूं न फसो तुम
नई विचारधारा का आरंभ करो
हताश या निराश हुए बिन, लड़ना प्रारंभ करो।

जब-जब इस रुह ने हार मान्ने कि कोशिशें कि
जिस्म ने फिर उसे जगाने कि साजिशें कि
तो युहीं तु टूट न
जुनून कि बुझि आग का फिर आरंभ कर
थक, मगर यूं हार न मान लड़ना फिर प्रारंभ कर।

दामन को तेरे यूं स्वच्छ रख कि दरपण भी शरमाये
कुछ कर ऐसा कि तेरा परचम विश्व में लहराये
तू बस अपने ज़मीर को ज़िन्दा रख
आरंभ कर
फल कि चिंता किए बिन नइ योजना के साथ लड़ना प्रारंभ कर।

कोई और नहीं

आज समस्याएँ सबको दिखती है
पर उपाय को कोई तैयार नहीं।

मिलती सबको है पर बिना मेहनत के
सफलता वो खैरात नहीं।

और बेशक तू बेताब है मंजिल पाने को
पर यकीन मान उस मुकाम के तू अभी काबिल नहीं।

सब्र रख अभी तेरा दौर नहीं
ताउम्र मंजिल तेरी होगी बस खुदको एसा बना जैसा कोई और
नहीं।

"वजूद रख एसा कि जहाँ तुझसे रूबरू हो
वक्त को तेरी जुस्तजू और तुझे भी तेरे वक्त कि आरज़ू हो"

Alisha Khan

68

Alisha khan is a lawyer writer and a social worker she has been a part of many anthologies and is from Karachi Pakistan.

Its life we need to face it
Maybe we are in the end game now
Or maybe it's just the beginning
Or maybe it's just the trailer
We never know
But one thing I know
That the Sun will shine again
The rain will be beautiful again
The loved ones will be together again
Its us who fight together
& Win together
Just look up in the sky and smile to say that
We all will come out of this very soon....
Because we are humans, that extraordinary species in the universe
who can fight anything with our love,
courage and pride....
The Sun Will Rise again!!!!
Soon...

Smile, my dear,
Don't have fear,
Let's forget the tears,
And be with your dears,
Smile, forget sadness,
Be with full of happiness,
Stay on peace,
Live fully on ease,
Work hard and smart,
Get up success, the true reward,
Have smile on your face,
Share it to others who have sad face!
Here no one care,
The world now is not fair,
Only you will be you,
No one at last will be with you!

Kirtika Bhatt

Kirtika Bhatt is an eighteen-year-old student interested in reading and writing.

Travail

Once upon a time, he was rejected for not being fit
The ball with the bat for a single run he could not hit
In every match he was told to sit
Everyone around him asked him to quit
He felt his life was struck in a pit
When everyone called him dumb wit
Ignoring everyone he used to pick up his kit
And tried to give his every bit
Until he made his skills lit
And his face full of zit
He pushed his every limit
And gracefully his flaws did he admit
There was nothing hampering his spirit
And finally, success paid him a visit
Gone were the days when he was called a gait
Now every tournament for him was a game of profit

Supriya Mukherjee

Supriya Mukherjee is a 19 years old girl, born on October 25th, 2002 in Ramgarh, Ranchi, Jharkhand. Currently She is pursuing BSc. in Biotechnology from Marwari College, Ranchi. She completed her 10th and 12th from Ramgarh. She aims to become a researcher in her life so that she could contribute to nation. During her school life, she won gold, silver and bronze medals in Judo. It is actually a great achievement and due to that she carries spirit of sportsmanship which leads her to face every situation in a positive way.

कुछ कर गुजरने की उम्मीद अभी जारी है,
ज़ख्म भरे हाथों से अल्फाजों को सजाना बाकी है।
लिख देंगे अपनी दास्ताँ -ए-जिन्दगी हम,
सब्र कर मैदान में आना अभी बाकी है।

<u>कोशिश करता जा।</u>

कुछ करना है तो डटकर चल,
मगर दुनिया से हटकर चल।

जब तक तुझे हासिल ना हो मंज़िल,
कोशिश करता जा हासिल होगा साहिल।

मुश्किल है मगर करना ज़रूरी है,
मंज़िल दूर है मगर पाना जरूरी है।

कोशिश करता जा हल जरूर निकलेगा,
आज नहीं तो कल तू जरूर निखरेगा।

कुछ ना मिला तो कुछ सीख जाओगे,
जिंदगी का अनुभव साथ ले जाओगे।

Sneha Sathyanathan

Sneha is a literature student. She will never accept her defeat very soon and will again and again come up with new ideas to overcome her problems. This happens only because of her self-motive thinking.

Self-Belief

Think in your own way;
stand in your own way;
walk in your own way;
so that many will follow your way.

Optimization

Interconnecting your own life situations
with one another,
will tell you
how lucky you are.

Akash Chaurasiya

This is Akash Chaurasiya from Azamgarh, living in Lucknow. He completed his intermediate from KV AMC Lucknow. He loves to write Hindi poems and English Articles.

मुझे फर्क नहीं पड़ता

तुम सोचते हो क्या मेरे बारे, सोचते रहो, फ़र्क नहीं पड़ता मुझे,
पागल बोलो, या शैतान, बोलते रहो, फ़र्क नहीं पड़ता मुझे,
परेशान तो मै हमेशा ही करूंगा, कभी लिखकर, कभी रातों मै जगा कर बातो से,
मुझे तुम बदल नहीं सकते, चाहे अलग करलो खुद से,
फ़र्क पड़ता नहीं मुझे...

मै अच्छा लिखूं या बुरा लिखूं, बुरे पे आप हस लेना, फ़र्क नहीं पड़ता,
मेरे बातें दिल पे लगे या दिल छू ले, आप पलटकर ज़वाब दीजिए,
दिल तोड़िए, तोड़िए गुरूर मेरा, पर मेरा आत्मविशवास ना हिला सकोगे,
फ़र्क पड़ता नहीं, जो चाहे तो आप कोशिश करके देख लीजिए...

ले चल तू तूफ़ान सांसों में, जो लाए आंसू उसके लिए तू सैलाब ला,
रख इरादे चट्टान से, कहने दे इन्हे, ये ज़माना हमेशा कहता है,
तू मेहनत कर, सुन मत इनकी, जी अपनी ज़िन्दगी,
सोना भी खरा बनता है, जो ज्यादा ताप सहता है...

खुद की सुनो, और सुनते रहो,
अपने काम, अपने दिमाग से करते रहो,
ज़िन्दगी एक बार मिली है, अपने हिसाब से जियो,
ज़माने की बाते नजरअंदाज करते रहो...

तुम अच्छा लिखोगे खुद के लिए, ये पढ़कर तुम्हारे लेखकीय का
दाम पूछेंगे,
तुम अच्छे काम करने जाओगे, ये तुमसे तुम्हारा धर्म और नाम पूछेंगे,
 इनका काम ही अडंगे लगाना, ये लगाते रहेंगे,
इनसे, इनकी लड़ाई में जीत गए तो, क्या मिला इनाम पूछेंगे...

Anshika Dutt

Anshika Dutt is a passionate writer who has been writing for 10 years now. Currently she is pursuing footwear designing. She also enjoys cooking and sports. She has received medals for writing in both school and college. According to her writing is the best way to express emotions.

The Dark Night Sky

Remember the times when the spirits flew high
The silence engulfing the world
The little tears in the eyes making the vision blurred
Looking up only the far-reaching night sky in sight
Telling the heart that it will be alright
The stars are shining bright
But they have to burn to give the light
The moon gives hope though it is far
Look closely the sun had even the moon scarred
The dark will always fade in the morning shine
This always shows that everything will one day be fine
The dawn cracks the silence of the night
The birds chirping making the morning bright
The fresh breeze whispering in the ear to get up
The bright blue sky making the dark thoughts disrupt
See through the darkness there is always light
The destination is not always in sight

Rabadiya Gopi D.

Student of Sardarkrushinagar Dantiwada Agriculture University, Gopi Rabadiya comes from Junagadh city of Gujarat. She is passionate about Agriculture . She is very attentive towards photography and sports. She is a national level player in various sports. She is highly attentive towards her religious beliefs. Most of her write ups are based on love and Nature's feel. Her poems are based on the fantasy of her life... She thinks that fantasy can create your life better and makes your world cheerful.

छोटी सी ख्वाईश रख

छोटी सी ख्वाईश रख,
खुद से ही जितने की नुमाईश रख,
विचारों को तेज घोड़े की रफतार रख,
विघ्न आये हजार तो भी मन मक्कम रख,
विस्वास की एक दौर हंमेशा साथ रख,
खुद की पहचान खुद से रख,
मंजिल की छबी साफ़ रख,
सुनाने वाले को दूर रख,
साथ देने वाले को करीब रख,
आस्मा छूने की एक बात रख,
मन में अपने एक ख्वाईश रख,
छोटी ही सही पर मंजिल अड़ग रख,
एक छोटी सी ख्वाईश रख,
खुद से ही जितने की नुमाईश रख...

Sneha B. Mankar

A 19 years old dynamic, ardent pen girl believes in the power of magical words. Sneha Mankar, the exploring wordsmith has cosenaristed anthology books like "Whisper of Hearts-1" and "Words That Stay Forever -1". She started her journey 4 years back when the changing world, people and ambient around her was affecting the way she thinks and act. And thus, she succeeded in giving voice to the wrestle of her agony and heartstrings. Her thoughts suffocating in skin made friends with pen and paper. And so she does believe that "Pen is a powerful gadget to expel thoughts."

Sometimes

Sometimes it's better to be alone.
To be alone and analyse yourself...
Thinking of all the good memories that you shared
with your family and your friends...
To be alone and thinking of all the bad things
you did to your known ones; knowingly or unknowingly...
Sitting alone; away from all sorts of thoughts;
positive or negative...
At a peaceful place.
Thinking about the times when you laughed
and smiled at your extreme and also cried to your fullest!
Thinking about all the good and bad times in your life;
all the betrayals, all the heartbreaks,
about all the people who pacified you,
all your accompanying and cooperative friends.
With all this, refresh your mind.
Because no one in this world is the best motivator
or soul-healer than you yourself!

J Vetri Michael Raj

Vetri Michael Raj J is an English literature graduate, pursuing his master degree in English literature and also he is a Carnatic music student. He loves the traditional writing and fanboy of Franz Kafka, Fyodor Dostoevsky and marcel Proust writings, but his works are unconventional. He is both bibliophile and cinephile. check out his blog @blogofvetri.home.blog. You can reach him by Instagram @vetrimichaelraj

Free Fallin'

I felt the strain in my back, it's getting onerous. My father and mother are not the same personalities I saw 15 years back. They don't smile at me nowadays. My dad with a baton in his hand, like a troop commander shouting at me. My mom, I thought she would never give up on me, but she did. I can't afford anything for my family neither support them, but I am fortunate to do household obligations.

Oh! It's a shame to tell about my love story, I'm not worth for it, all amours, busses, and cuddles closed down on the planned talks when it became very pressing, and my love had lost its vigor. Lots of breaks and screams, and it makes me nauseous, like a paranoid disorder.

Ok! What can I see outside of my home? Tycoon's son picking all shots, even if I have the potential to pull it, who can subsidize me? What damn thing can remain for me. Now I have to believe in God and religion. So I can shift my load on their shoulders.

Ruskin bond's 'The night train at Deoli' portrays the idea 'let go of something', I am striving to follow bond's idea of existence, and I am subletting all things pass, in the end, I am losing myself in the void.

My playlist is getting rusty, 'led zeppelin' is my only messiah who keeps me motivated. There's no voting for what I love. My passion, it's sealed and drowned in the ocean.

But somewhere in the corner of my heart says that 'just one more phase to go'. Maybe it's a pep talk for myself but

believed that all these things that I've been through are just random phase. There's no advantage for me in this world, only hard work will trigger me to the vast.

Falling is easy, but subsisting in this system is troublesome. I always select the difficult choices.

Shaheen Ansari

She is pursuing Masters in Microbiology. And the one who try to put her thoughts in words of her imaginary world with her unique viewpoint. She is a free soul of an utopia with a perspective of protopia. Her viewpoint to see the world have always been come up as the hog heaven were everything is just perfect and fulfilled. To connect with her through e-mail shahiin.ansarii@gmail.com and also Instagram - shahin_ansari_22.

Work On Myself I Do

Nowadays we just encounter many events in life that could be traumatic, worrying about future and feels like perturb. And we just lose oneself in the competition of being best which leads to unresolved issues. At that time, we should work on our own self for our contentment. One's own happiness also called as Self-love. As a person meets so many uncertainties and dreadful incidents in their life that leads to make them feel lonely, depressed, blank or deprived from everyone.

At that time what I actually want for me is, inner peace within myself that could be felt without depending on others for my happiness. Just by focusing on calmness in self and by ignoring the worldly hustle and bustle around us. Sometimes I just get tired of all the bullshit going on in our life or around it. At that moment everything gets jumbled as in, Heart wants to escape from there, somewhere where everything is right and Mind always reminds of that happenings again and again which makes us me more distress. And that may leads to pretending being someone who I am not and just try to be happy with something which I am not otherwise I would be unable to cope up with the life which is easy though hard to live.

Inner peace is not something that someone will get from avoiding people but that will get by knowing oneself more and exploring own self. As there would be some situations where I completely lost myself as well as lost the track of life and everything seems gloomy and felt like completely blackout. In that time, just give yourself time to find what inner me wants? And I think, Of all the things I have waited for, tranquillity of my mind which was lost in the worldly hurry-scurry, made me more confused about me, What was I? How was I? Am I doing great? Am I doing what I wanted?

Have I achieved my goals? Am I lost in the way? Will I get succeeded? Will I have better future ahead?

And I think most of the questions have been answered by myself, by just giving time to oneself and that cleared my head out. Sometimes I also experienced getting negative vibes around me that made me feel low or inferior and ends up making me questioning to myself. I just feel that, serenity is like the light within us, which we shouldn't get it dim by the winds of bad influence around us, just protect it with the shield of righteousness and let the brightness of our inner shine reach more distant that may awaken the goodness in the minds of dark.

Priyanka Varma

She is Priyanka Varma studying Masters of Pharmacy from Visakhapatnam. She is a National and Central Zonal Sports Player along with being a Classical Dancer and an Artist. Along with these, she is also a poetess fond of writing her thoughts. she believes that "If You Don't See Your Worth You'll Always Choose People Who Don't See It Either. When Your Self Esteem Rises, Your Life Follows".

Confidence

Do not undermine your worth by comparing yourself with others,
It is because we are different that each of us is special.
I promise myself-
To be so strong that nothing can disturb my peace of mind.
To talk health, happiness, and prosperity to every person I meet.
To make all my friends feel that there is something worthwhile in them.
To look at the sunny side of everything, and make my optimism come true.
To think only of the best, to work only for the best and to expect only the best.
To be just as enthusiastic about the success of others as I am about my own.
To forget the mistakes of the past and press on to the greater achievements of the future.
To wear a cheerful expression at all times and give a smile to every living creature I meet.
To give so much time to improving myself that I have no time to criticize others.
To be too large for worry, too noble for anger, too strong for fear, and too happy to permit the presence of trouble.
To think well of myself and to proclaim this fact to the world, not in loud words, but in great deeds.
To live in the faith that the whole world is on my side, so long as I am true to the best that is in me.

Don't Quit

Things go wrong as they sometimes will,
Life is strange with its twists and turns,
Often the goal might be nearer than it seems,
Our greatest weakness lies in giving up
You only fail when you stop trying
Rest if you must, but don't quit.
It takes years of preparation for one moment of glory
Never hold your head down,
Never say you can't,
Never limit yourself,
And
Never stop believing.
Success is failure turned inside out.
If you want to give up,
Close your eyes and remember
Why you started.
Don't give up,
Hold On Pain Ends
- HOPE

Rashmi Sri

श्रीमती रश्मि श्री जी बिहार की रहने वाली हैं। जो अपने घर के साथ साथ अपने लेखन को भी समय देती हैं। वह ज्यादातर जीवन और प्रेरणा से जुड़ी रचनाएं लिखती हैं। वह स्वयं में एक प्रेरणा का स्रोत हैं। उनकी रचनाएं वाकई काफ़ी प्रेरणादायक हैं।

खुद पर भरोसा और बस आगे के सारे रास्ते आसान। खुद पर भरोसा करना ही एकमात्र ऐसा मार्ग है जो हमें सफलता की ओर ले जाता है यहां असंभव कुछ भी नहीं...

जहाँ दूसरे कर सकते हैं वहां हम क्यूँ नहीं? हमें ज्यादा कुछ नहीं करना होता है, बस हमें हमारे आस-पास से कुछ ऐसी बातें खुद में समेटनी होती है जो हमे सकारात्मक ऊर्जा दे। बस एक लक्ष्य निर्धारित करनी होती है। खुद के भरोसे से प्राप्त की गई सफलता इसकी व्याख्या मुमकिन ही नहीं। हमारी जिंदगी किसी चुनौती से कम नहीं होती है। इसे हमें स्वीकार करना ही होता है। वर्ना हमारा इस दुनिया में कोई अस्तित्व ही नहीं होगा हमें अपने जीवन को सफल और खूबसूरत बनाना होता है। इसके लिए हमें हमारे ख्वाबों का पीछा करना होता है। गिरते- संभलते कभी कभी हम गलतियां भी करते हैं ऐसा मेहसूस करते हैं कि हम टूट चुके हैं। उस वक्त हमे खुद को संभालना होता है।

नए नए अच्छे-बुरे अनुभवों के साथ खुद को साबित करना होता है। हमें खुद के लिए एक बेहतर इंसान बनना होता है। कभी कभी हम सोचते हैं क्या हम खुद को नियंत्रित कर सकते हैं अगर परिस्थिति हमारे विपरित हो शायद हां शायद ना आंखें बंद करो तो दूर दूर तक अंधेरा ही अंधेरा...

दूर दूर तक कोई रोशनी नहीं हम चीख रहे होते हैं चिल्ला रहे होते हैं। फिर भी हमें हमारी आवाज सुननी होती है। हमें इन्हीं चीखें मे से खुद की आवाज पहचानी होती है। हमें ये सोचने की जरूरत होती है कि आखिर हमें चाहिए क्या वही एकमात्र आवाज होती है जो हमे सफलता की ओर ले जाती है।

Sakshi Jain

She is Sakshi Jain, writer by passion and student by profession. Since childhood she is fond of writing her inner thoughts and always try to bring change in society with her words.

Let Go Of Perfection

Hey Inner self,
I know you are feeling low,
Everything seems like arrow and bow,
Your heart wants to speak out,
But you are unable to say loud,
Things are looking like scary nightmare,
But at all who cares,
In crowded days and lonely nights,
You are doing self-fights,
Stop your self-doubt session,
Don't ask for validation,
Just try to seek satisfaction,
And let go of perfection.

Alone

Being alone never meant
That you are lonely,
You are your
Bestest friend only,
World is full of devil's and demons
It's hard to find good in someone,
Try to carry your own baggage
You know this is the real savage,
From twinkle nursery stories
To high-school education,
We heard lonely is only lion
Make your path a perfect picture,
Because of you world will get best future.

Ankitha P Menon

Co-author is Ankitha P Menon. She is from Mumbai. Has graduated from science stream. She is writing since last 7 months. Her interests are reading, writing and music. Her dream is to follow her passion and in future write her own novel.

Safar Ek Zindagi Ki...

Kuch kehte hai chal aaj apne aap se..
Kuch sachh, kuch Anjaan baatein...
Kaha hai joh beeti hai Zindagi mein...
Phir bhi lagta hai kuch baaki hai Iss Safar mein...
Kabhi durr se hi raahat milee...
Paas aane par baicheni si lage...
Ruthee hue ko manaa na pade...
Aisi bhalaa hum wajaah kyu de...
Kahi hui baaton ko sunkar bhi ansunaa kare…
Kehne waale wahi log hai, joh phir se kehne ko mile...
Dard agar uthe chahein woh dil mein ho ya aatma mein...
Kehte hai raasta wahi kaaton bharaa joh dard de aur manzil
bhi hume...
Kehte hai kisi ka saath ho toh safar apna sa Lagta...
Kya pata woh apna sa ajnabee tumhaare intezaar mein toh
Nahi...
Tootkar bikhar na jaana Safar mein kaheen...
Aankhein uthaa aur dekh.. Ghar tera do kadam durr toh
nahi...
Jab Dil mein sawaalon ka toofan bharaa ho, toh baahar
nahi… Khojna apne dil ke andar kahi...
Jawaabon ka samandar hai bharaa...
Tu zaraa apne dil ko tatolkar toh dekh Sahi....
Raat ke andhere ko na dekh ae musafir, taaron ka hai lagaa
mela aur chaand bhi mehfil mein hai wahi... Jab saweraa
hoga tab yeh jannat pookaregi tujhe...ki aa dekh tere swaagat
mein khud sunehra rang khili hui...
Tootkar bikhar na jaane safar mein kaheen... Aankhein
uthaakar dekh... Ghar tera do kadam durr toh nahi...
Pyaasa hai tu agar toh nadiyon Ka bahaanv hai... Bhooka hai
agar toh pedon ki pukaar hai...
Thak jaayein raaston mein chalkar toh tham jaana wahi...

Kudrat ne banaaya hai yeh ghar... Pyaar aur umeedon se bharaa... kuch daer tu rukk jaa wahi...
Yeh na teherna sikhaata hai, na mudkar waapas apne kadam peeche ki taraf Lena... Joh tune nazar palti toh kahi tere kadam dagmagaa toh gaye nahi...
Tootkar bikhar na jaana Safar mein kaheen... Aankhein utha aur dekh... Ghar tera kuch kadam durr toh nahi...
Kachchi hai sadak abhi Tu Inn raaston ko parakh toh sahi...
Kya pata kal yehi raastein Teri raahon ke pakki sadak toh nahi...
Chalna hai zaroori, milti hai manzil usse hi...joh na haar maane, joh na kadam Roke.. himmat ki misaal
Tu bankar dikhaa, phir tu hi sahi...
Safar Ek Zindagi Ki...
Kuch kehte chal aaj apne aapse...
Tootkar bikhar na jaana Safar mein kaheen...
Aankhein uthaa kar tu dekh... Safar khatam... Teri ghar ki chaokhat mein tu hai abhi.

Ankita Dey

Ankita Dey, the author of Blessed With Words, is a student of Science from India, pursuing her dreams. She has always been passionate about writing poetry and stories since she was 8 years old. She never gave up her passion for writing; in fact, she always says that writing accompanied her in her hard times. Besides writing, she is also a great dancer and a book- lover. She loves painting as well. Her preferred genres for writing poetry are love, life, horror, mystery, revenge, and pain. You can find her book on Amazon.

Letting Go Of You

You never really let me grow,
'Cause you have never loved me,
So, you tried to let me down...

I still remember the time,
When you said that you were mine,
And will forever be...

I let you burn my soul,
You knew you owned my whole,
Was it why you didn't leave a piece of me alive?

I had to let go of you, to find 'me',
To become the girl I used to be,
To nourish the goodness in my heart I lost...

Yes, I could never find the pieces, you had burnt,
But still the lost ones had returned,
And you can't take those back from me now...

Piece by piece, I will let myself grow,
Even more than you last saw,
And soon, I'll move on...

Sharmistha Kar

Sharmistha Kar, from Siliguri West Bengal is a writer both by profession and passion. She has been working as a freelance content writer over the past five years. She has done her masters in English from North Bengal University and holds a professional degree in Nutritionist from Ireland. Apart from the above, she is also a teacher who loves imparting the little knowledge that she has. She is the co-author of 65+ anthologies. Her writings have been well-known over various social media platforms.

My Anxiety : My Worst Enemy

Every person has some sorts of fear inbuilt within their minds. Fear may vary from person to person depending on their mental health conditions. Fear can even become worst at a point which can even make a living person feel dead. Anxiety is my biggest fear. The only barrier that comes every time between me and my success lowering the level of my self-confidence. Anxiety is one of the most common mental disorders. People suffering from the illness prefer to keep it hidden within them being afraid of the fact that other might not understand them or laugh on their illness. After fighting the battle with the same for the longest time period, I finally decided to overcome it. I made my inner self understand that one illness cannot be more powerful than your dreams.

Emotional discomfort is a very normal universal experience, let's not fear and fight it back together with utmost confidence.

Ranu Manjhi 'Sanskriti'

Miss Ranu Manjhi 'Sanskriti' was born on 20th September 2001. She is from Sagar, (M.p.).she is lives at Rehli. Her father's name is Mr. Ramgopal Manjhi and her mother's name Mrs. Prema Manjhi. Ranu is a person with soft and pure heart who is always ready to help others. She is smart with many talents and mostly a creative human being. Ranu writes from the heart. She was having passion for poetry, singing, dancing and painting. "Enjoy every moment of life....until it become memories...collect memories as like MEETHI YAADEIN."

<u>सिर्फ तुम आगे बढ़ते चलो</u>

कोई रोकेगा नहीं रास्ता,
तुम जुनून बचाकर चलो!

अंधेरे में रोशनी न सही,
तुम रोशन रास्ते करते चलो!

जिंदगी में कुछ ख्वाब बुनो,
उम्मीदो को साथ रखकर चलो!

छाँव की तलाश छोड़ दो,
धूप में तुम तपकर चलो!

छोटी-छोटी खुशियो में,
जिंदगी को ढूढकर तुम चलो!

राह में कोई साथ न सही,
तुम अकेले आगे बढ़कर चलो!

जिंदगी में मीठे लम्हों को,
तुम हमेशा साथ बुनकर चलो!

रंग बदलती हुई जिंदगी में,
तुम अपना नया रंग भरकर चलो!

मंजिल दूर ही सही,
तुम कदम आगे बढ़ाकर चलो!

मुश्किल सफर ही सही,
खुद पर भरोसा बनाकर चलो!
भीड़ तो बहुत हैं, पर...
तुम नयी राह बनाकर सिर्फ आगे बढ़ते चलो!

Keerthana

Keerthana hails from Chennai, Tamil Nadu A girl of sixteen running towards her dream, Full of Hope, finding her happiness in the smallest things. She's a blend of emotions trying to express it through her writings. Her main goal is to motivate people around her and spread positivity with smiles forever. You can find her writings relatable @quotes_by_girly_writer

Optimism: "The Peak of Life"

Life is all about facing ups & Downs in every situation , but every time when you fall down, You learn something new and you will get an unforgettable experience!! After gaining all the experiences you will be tired of trying. But if you remain stubborn not to give up and get back up you will succeed with your hard work and efforts. You will feel like flying in the sky with loads of enjoyment , likely to be the happiest person in the world. That's why I tell life is beautiful. Whenever you are sad just think about someone who has no shelter , no food , no clothing. When compared, we are blessed. We are the happiest person in the world as God has selected and provided us with the gifted abilities. We are gifted as we are able to enjoy and feel all the little things happening around which makes our life beautiful. After rain when you find the rainbow you just admire the beauty of it along with its cloudy climate. In the early morning when the rooster cocks you admire the minute hidden beautiful things which gives you the feeling that you are gifted!!

Every day is a new beginning. Wakeup with a ray of positivity that you could achieve something great and make the day favourable to you. Impossible is nothing, just excuses meant for lazy people. Excuses and reasons are common and only losers keep asking and searching. Failure is not a very rare thing which only happens to you. It came to each and every successful person who took failure as a motivation and not as dead end. They never think of quitting cuz they wanted their dreams to come true. They wanted to see their dream destination called success. With the consistent hard work and sleepless nights they have achieved . Work for what you want and nothing comes easy. Remember things which are gotten easily has not a big value. Consistency is the key to success. Problems are not too big; we are too small to handle them. There are people whose life is greatest problem and still they survive . Problems should bring changes in us. They break us, heal us, damage our soul forever. But finally, we become better stronger and powerful. The best lessons are taught with painful feelings and with pain. Make yourself engaged. Make yourself as a role model and make others to choose you as a role model. Never follow other's path. Create your own path and make it define. Make sure that consistency in your hardest tasks even in bad times, you should do it which will bring up colourful results and helps to taste the sweetest destination called success.

Procrastination leads to failure. It puts our energy down and makes our mind dumb.

Payal Kamdi

Payal Kamdi is from Maharashtra. She is a passionate writer and surrounded by thoughts. Personally, she believes that Self-motivation doesn't work until and less you try to beat in your breathe.

I am not perfect creature
For I am born as a human
I am immature
I am impulsive
I am arrogant
I am stubborn
I am childish
I am careless
I am not flawless.
I do mistakes but that's how learn
That's how I grow and try to do new
I try to find my own path.
Along every broken piece I suffer
It lets me afford that pain which makes me strong, stronger
For others I am stupid
Coz they are others not mine.
Falling too hard on stone doesn't make me hurt
Every soft thing is wrapped in a special place
That's like is my heart hold me tightly into its breaths.

Harshita Verma

Co-author Harshita Verma is a writer from Lucknow. She has completed her graduation in commerce stream. She has been writing poetry for the last few years as her passion. She wants to be a novelist in future.

Value Yourself Motivate Yourself

Before valuing others start valuing yourself
It will bring self confidence in your life
It will bring self-respect for your identity
It will bring trust in yourself before anyone else.

Before taking decisions believe yourself
It will bring self-sufficiency in your decisions
It will bring mindfulness in your life
It will bring courage in your heart.

Before pursuing the dreams learn to build a strong self
esteem
It will bring hope to reach the goals
It will bring positivity in the path
It will bring encouragement at each step.

Always value yourself before anything else
Because you are the only one to help yourself before
anyone else.

Ankita Nahar

Ankita Nahar, physically she lives in Rajasthan but heartly live in everywhere. She is too much passionate about writing. She has always found comfort in words, and that's what attracts everyone. Writing is her therapy, she writes what she feels and experiences in her life.

बहुत निभाए रिश्ते,
अब खुद से प्यार करने की बारी हैं
बहुत मनाया लोगों को,
अब खुद को मनाने की बारी हैं ।
बहुत गलतियां भुलाई लोगों की,
अब लोगों को भुलाने की बारी हैं।
बहुत किया सब के लिए,
अब कर्ज चुकाने की बारी हैं ।
बहुत प्यार किया लोगो से,
अब खुद से प्यार करने की बारी हैं
देखते ही देखते बहुत बदल गए लोग
अब मेरी बारी हैं, अब सिर्फ मेरी बारी हैं |

लोग मुझे अक्सर पागल, दीवानी,
बावली बुला लेते हैं
क्योंकि मुझे खुद से बेहद प्रेम हैं...
और ये सिर्फ बोलने के लिए है...
ऐसा भी नहीं है...
जिंदगी ने बहुत कुछ सिखाया है...
तब जाकर इतना समझ आया है...
खुद से प्यार करने में जो मजा हैं...
वो कहीं और आ ही कैसे सकता है...
अच्छा तुम ही सोचो जरा
जो इंसान खुद से प्यार नहीं कर सका...
वो दूसरों से कैसे प्यार कर पायेगा ???
जो इंसान खुद को खुश नहीं रख सका...
वो दूसरों को कैसे खुश रख पाएगा ???
जो इंसान खुद के लिए जी नहीं सका...
वो इंसान दूसरों के लिए कैसे जी पायेगा...
तो सोचो और बताओ जरा...
की जो खुद से प्यार नहीं कर पाया...
वो जिंदगी में क्या ही कर पायेगा ???

Rahul Singh

Rahul Singh from Chitrakoot, Uttar Pradesh
Contact us Email- bhairahul113@gmail.com.
Insta- @adhure__khwab

आप सफलता तब तक नहीं प्राप्त कर सकते जब तक
आप में असफल होने का साहस न हो...!!

स्टेटस मोबाईल का हो या
ज़िंदगी का हो,
पर ऐसा रखना की लोगों को
कॉपी करना ही पड़े।

अगर आप समय पर अपनी गलतियों को स्वीकार नहीं करते है तो
आप एक और गलती कर बैठते है।
आप अपनी गलतियों से तभी सीख सकते है जब आप अपनी
गलतियों को स्वीकार करते है।

हमें किसी भी ख़ास समय के लिए इन्तजार नहीं करना चाहिए बल्कि
अपने हर समय को ख़ास बनाने की पूरी तरह से कोशिश करनी
चाहिए।

बीता हुआ कल अगर वर्तमान पर नकारात्मक प्रभाव डालने लगे तो
बीते हुये कल को जहर समझ कर त्याग देना चाहिये!

अगर जिंदगी में कुछ बुरा हो तो थोड़ा
सब्र रखना,
क्योंकि रोने के बाद हंसने
का मजा ही कुछ और आता है !

पैर को लगने वाली चोट संभल कर चलना सिखाती है और
मन को लगने वाली चोट समझदारी से जीना सिखाती हैं।

आंखों में नींद बहुत है पर सोना नहीं है
यही समय है कुछ करने का मेरे दोस्त इसे खोना नही है।

अगर आप सही हो तो कुछ भी साबित
करने की कोशिश मत करो,
बस सही बने रहो गवाही वक़्त खुद दे देगा।

क्यों रुक जाते हो 4 दिन की मेहनत के बाद,
अरे वक्त लगता है बीज को फसल बनने में।

आज तुझ पर हंस रहे हैं जो,
वही लोग कल को तेरा गुणगान करेंगे ...
कर के दिखा दे कोई कमाल,
तो तुझ पर सब अभिमान करेंगे

तेरे खिलाफ़ क्या तूफ़ान,
क्या आँधी और क्या सूनामी करेंगे
आज बाधा बनके जो खड़े हैं,
कल तुझे ये सलामी करेंगे।

Abhinav Sharma

What life means to you at the age when you cross your teens...
Well, for any ambitious person life is chasing a dream. A dream well that's a powerful word!
 Chasing a dream ain't easy cause it's takes hell of a fight and so many people give up
Before giving remember why you started.
Let the fire burn your soul cause if you wanna shine like sun you gotta burn like it.
You're more POWERFUL than you even know! YOU CAN CHANGE THE WORLD with your dream. But it only requires you to get out of your comfort zone and unleash your inner lion!
It requires you to let that lion out its cage, IT REQUIRES YOU TO CHASE YOUR DREAMS NO MATTER WHAT. Now listen
You will get knocked down many times chasing your dreams, you will feel like you don't have the energy to get back up. You don't have the STRENGTH to get back up. You will feel like giving up is the only option.
When you're hit, when you've been knocked down by life that's when it's time to hit back!
THAT'S WHEN IT'S TIME TO HIT BACK! Never give up on your dreams

Abhay Sinha

Abhay Sinha is currently a student. He is an active listener, and has participated in national debate. He is pursuing science as his primary stream. He is also a sports enthusiast. He loves to write and travel.

Run Free

So, go and run free with the angels
Dance around the golden clouds
For the lord has chosen you too be with him
And we should feel nothing but proud

Although he has taken you from us
and our pain lifetime will last
your memory will never escape us
but makers glad for the time we did have

Your face well always be hidden
Deep inside our hearts
Each precious moment you gave us
Shall never, ever depart

So, go and run free with the angels
As they sing so tenderly
And please be sure to tell them
To take good care of you for me.

Be Proud

Be proud of how
you've been
handling these past months.
They silent battles
you fought
The moments you
had to humble
Yourself, wiped
Your own tears
And pat yourself on the back
Celebrate your Strength

Somesh Kumar Jha

Pursuing B.Tech in Electrical Domain from Gautam Buddha University, Greater Noida, Delhi NCR.
"Having goal isn't enough to succeed, but you have to be smart enough so that you win, where the chances of your Success are quite low".

A Word Of Motivation

Love your life, love the way you live
No one can stay in your life like an eternal olive
Don't think, she will come one day
Be happy with what you have today
Think you don't need her in your life
Take a nap and create your own paradise
Just be calm and quiet
Think bright in the night's void.

Khushi Patil

This is Khushi Patil from Shahada, Maharashtra. She's pursuing masters degree in computer science from Shahada. A girl who loves magical spark of line on holding the air of positivism. she has worked as co-author in 5+ anthologies and process for more . She observes and feels everything by heart, spreading lots of positivity and colourful love. And she's loves to read LOVE HOPE MAGIC BY Ashish Bagrecha sir dancing is her dream and loves to write poems. Insta handle: khuushi_patil3521.

जिंदगी बड़ी अजीब है

जहां जीने के लिए वजह है
वहां मरने कि तरस है
जहां रिश्तों को संभालने की चाह है
पर वहीं कहीं रिश्तों में घुठन कि राह है
छुटते है यहां पक्के से पक्के धागें
फैसलों कि आड़ में लोग रिश्तों से है भागे
जिंदगी में यहां बड़े दर्द है
छुटकर भी ना छुटे यहां रिश्तों के कर्जे है
साथ हर किसी का है
पर सहारा तो सिर्फ जिंदगी तेरा है
जहां हर सांस जीने के लिए फनाह है
यहां हर वक्त हर पल बड़ा सुना सुना है
जी रहे हैं यहां सब दर्द संभाले हुए
नजाने क्युं बैचेन हो जाते हैं
यहां कहीं दिल धड़कनों के लिए
लिए चलते हैं जिंदगी लिए
हर वक्त डगमगाए हुए

Ami Patel

She is Ami Patel from Ankleshwar. 25 years old. She is writer, poet and book reviewer. She loves travelling. Her writing comes out of her feelings of her deepest relationships and its purity. She is also available on YouTube to share her views and writing. She works in human resource department. She appreciates life with its all perspectives.

You can give her review about her writing on instagram @amipatel95

It is easy to make your children modern and attractive. Make them tough and problem solver. Make them self-confident and innovative. Make them ask more questions. Make them humble. Tell them truth and facts. Tell them that it is not easy to earn when you belong to poor family. Help those people and be kind to them. Speak truth even if it is hard to say. Don't get in those people who want you to do as they say and do what you want. Do what feels right. Don't make life materialistic and explore new everyday. Tell them that life is short. Motivate them to do those things which feels impossible at first. Make them brave and intelligent. Tell them how your country has survived and why people are dying for you on border. Make him realise that meaning of life is to give. Motivate him to do those things which keep their hearts happy, not others eyes.

Bhavika Dhiraj Sindhi

Bhavika Dhiraj Sindhi is a 25-year-old
creative writer. She belongs to Turkey an Indian writing
from abroad due to her passion in writing. a curious girl
A wanderer who likes to explore new things and places a
hard-headed but soft-hearted.
She uses her pen as a best friend to speak her feelings...
Believes only love can make this place a better to survive...!

Unbroken And Brave You Shine...!

Every flower has a fragrance of its own...
Just because the other person can't smell it doesn't mean you aren't fragrant full,
You bloom and shine in your own unique way,
Struggling hard with the wind, snow and the sunlight to grow...
Yet not uttering a single word to any,
Everything may not be easy but not everyone can do it if you try...
Yes, you have the power my soul
Yes, yes you are unique in your own way.
Many will come many will go,
Until you aren't successful,
People will speak,
Let the dirty mouth speak,
But don't lose your struggles of the nights and hard work will be paid of one day...
You will be the shining star.
Because each one has one day,
But can only win if you believe in yourself,
Yes, my soul You can do it.
You ain't that weak.
Our life is a big puzzle,
Never do you know when will you turn,
Yes, believe in yourself,
Even when your shadow leaves you apart,
Your heart will pump and you will breathe,
Learn the process because you aren't meant to quit
Hold on, people are here to break,
You aren't that weak...
A diamond is known by its shine
It's okay to be dull someday,

Because you need to polish your skill,
To the gem you are unique and you meant to shine...
To quit is not your thing...!
You'd summoned the thunder,
Standing strong and beautiful
Yes, you can win...
Taking the talks of poisonous people, you crying that you dying...
Noo noo , Little soul you're brave ,
It's just a phase...
You are meant to shine
The rainbow and the dark clouds will move someday...
Just smile and let them stay confused...
To the strong like a warrior
You have come this far...
You cannot let go from this stage,
Thy you shall shine...!
Just hold on and believe in yourself
It's shall pass
Making you shine...
The fierce in you kept you going,
Yes, little soul you're are bright and unbroken...!
Thy shining in the moonlight too...!

Flairs and Glairs, a platform by a student for the students. We are esteemed youth struggling to carve out our path for our future and we follow a basic mindset Since everyone is not born with all-round skills. Joining hands with people who are born to execute it with perfection is the best way to evolve. Self-Evolution is the need of the hour but, evolving as a community is what we strive for. The initiative as kickstarted by, Founder- Mr. Shubham Shah with the motive to utilize the skillset and talent of writing has now a team of 10+ people who are actively participating into newer forms of learning and discovering talents among youngsters. We Provide platform and services like Publishing opportunities, Open mics, Workshops, Hands-on training. Operating with Brand Name of Flairs and Glairs (Publication House), we offer the chance of elevating a passionate writer to an esteemed author With Brand name Teekhe Zasbaaat. We bring to you an opportunity to get accustomed with the Public Speaking and Presenting of Thoughts along with regular challenges to brush up your inking spirit. The newest initiative to extend our services we introduced in a new writing Platform- The Glittering Fables and Ink Over Tears.

We Choose to Fly Like A Falcon than to be

a Leg Pulling Crab.

To Know More: Infoline – 7781900870
Mail Us At-
flairsandglairs@gmail.com / info@flairsandglairs.in
Or Visit is at
www.flairsandglairs.com / www.flairsandglairs.in
Social Handles- @flairsandglairs @teekhezasbaaat